Praise for *THE CHRISTMAS NOTE*

A warm and inspiring story. Give it to your children, mothers, and teachers. Spread it around! I know I will.
— **JOHNNY CASH**

Children and grownups alike will love this luminous look into the past—and Skeeter's childhood memory holds a gentle lesson for us all. Vivid, real writing and fine art.
— **LEE SMITH,** author of *The Devil's Dream*

Reading this story makes us all appreciate not only the true meaning of Christmas, but the real beauty of faith, family, and a sweet, innocent imagination.
— **VINCE GILL**

In THE CHRISTMAS NOTE, *Skeeter Davis and Cathie Pelletier share the secret of turning a stumbling block into a stepping stone. What a special gift, at Christmas or any other season. A beautiful, touching, and inspiring story!*
— **BILL ANDERSON**

Nothing is as Christmas as a story that leaves us in awe of the joy that emerges from tender pain. And THE CHRISTMAS NOTE *is that story. Brilliantly written, beautifully illustrated, this is Christmas in its timeless celebration of the heart.*
— **TERRY KAY,** author of *To Dance with the White Dog*

This is the most touching, most interesting Christmas story I've ever read. Thank you for sharing this beautiful book with everyone!
— **PORTER WAGONER**

Written with humility, honesty, and sincerity. Skeeter Davis and Cathie Pelletier have turned a childhood memory into a precious gift to the children of this world. THE CHRISTMAS NOTE *should be in every stocking. It's wonderful!*
— **JEANNE PRUETT**

I loved this book from cover to cover. It is so full of love and compassion. I recommend THE CHRISTMAS NOTE!
— **CHET ATKINS**

THE CHRISTMAS NOTE *is a wonderful gift. It reminds us all how blessed we are, no matter who we are.* — **GARTH BROOKS**

This story captures, with grace and simplicity, an important moment of illumination in a young girl's life. And the bluebird sings. — **SISSY SPACEK,** actress, *Coal Miner's Daughter*

Christmas is a blessing, and so is this dear little book. — **REBECCA WELLS,** author of *Divine Secrets of the Ya-Ya Sisterhood*

We loved THE CHRISTMAS NOTE *because it's the kind of book we like to read to our children. It's a story of a family sharing their experiences and traditions, and making memories that last a lifetime.* — **SHARON WHITE AND RICKY SCAGGS**

THE CHRISTMAS NOTE *is a heartwarming story of a family who was far richer in their love for each other than in material possessions. It was a blessing to us, and we know your family will love it too.* — **THE WHITES (BUCK, SHARON, AND CHERYL)**

A new Christmas classic. Not a word or sparkling image is out of place. This sweet book will be read and reread for years to come. A holiday tradition. Simply unforgettable. — **ELIZA CLARK,** author of *Miss You Like Crazy*

As I sat reading THE CHRISTMAS NOTE *I returned to a simple, more truthful time. And it cheered my heart. Good reading. Great lesson.* — **JESSI COLTER JENNINGS**

THE CHRISTMAS NOTE *will soften any heart at Christmastime. This tender tale of the bittersweet experiences of a young girl growing up poor and learning the true value of Christmas is both touching and lasting. Share this story with your own kids: they'll never forget it.* — **STEVEN WOMACK,** author of *Chain of Fools* and winner of the Edgar Award

ACKNOWLEDGMENTS:

This story is based on an actual event in Skeeter Davis's life. However, poetic license was taken wherever necessary for the sake of the story.

Grateful thanks from NASHVILLE BOOKS to the following good souls who did various duties to see this book on its way: Tom Viorikic, for Herculean labors; Justine Honeyman, for her own hard work; artist Russell Bradshaw, and photographer Scott Kemmerer, for their technical assistance; Jim Veatch, for various tasks; Martha Trachtenberg, for the chore of copyediting; Chris Vetetoe, Teresa Cox, Debbie Meisinger, and American Corporate Literature, Inc., for going the extra mile; Carl and Margaret Ann Hileman, for support; Lindsay and Jennifer Hesselmeyer, for the inspiration that comes from children.

Grateful acknowledgements to Eddy Arnold for "Will Santy Come to Shanty Town," written by Eddy Arnold, Ed Nelson Jr., and Steve Nelson, © 1949 by Warner/Chappell Music, Inc.

Publisher's Cataloging in Publication

Davis, Skeeter.

   The Christmas note / by Skeeter Davis & Cathie Pelletier; with illustrations by Carl E. Hileman

   p. cm.

   ISBN 0-9660776-0-1

   1. Christmas—United States. 2. Country musicians—United States—Biography. 3. Davis, Skeeter. I. Pelletier, Cathie. II. Hileman, Carl E. III. Title.

GT4986.A1D375 1997   394.2663

FIRST EDITION

Paintings are 24 x 30 oils on canvas.

Colophon: *Old Birch Tree*, Allagash, Maine
Designed by John Hafford, Northland Studio, Caribou, Maine

Printed by American Corporate Literature, Inc., Nashville, Tennessee
Bound by Nicholstone, Inc., Nashville, Tennessee

The Christmas Note

by *Cathie Pelletier* [signature]

Skeeter Davis & Cathie Pelletier

Illustrated by Carl E. Hileman *[signature]*

NASHVILLE BOOKS, Nashville, Tennessee

DEDICATIONS:

SKEETER DAVIS: To my brothers and sisters, James (Buddy), Shirley (Poochie), Harold (Boze), Dean (Punkin), Carolyn Sue (Doozie); and in loving memory of my parents, William and Sarah Penick, and my youngest sister, Leona Ann (Hoopers); also in special memory of my grandparents, Luther and Leona Naomi Penick. My love and dedication to my Savior, Jesus Christ, who teaches me the lessons of love, joy, forgiveness, and peace. He gives us Christmas and Santa Claus! And I want to thank Cathie from the bottom of my heart for making this dream a reality. Also thanks to those she chose—especially Carl and Tom—to help bring this book to all our children of the world.

CATHIE PELLETIER: For Ethel and Louis Pelletier (mother and daddy) in memory of those cold Christmases in Allagash, Maine; Jonah Hafford, my grade-school teacher, who always brought the holidays to life; Emma Grace Pelletier, celebrating her first Christmas. And to Skeeter, who gave me poetic license because she understands.

CARL E. HILEMAN: In memory of Susie Hileman, my grandmother.

I grew up in Dry Ridge, Kentucky, back in the days of oil lamps and candles. I was born Mary Frances, but my granddaddy Martin Luther Penick named me *Skeeter*. He said I was fast as a water bug, always skeeting here and there. In my family we had a lot of unusual nicknames anyway. My sisters were called *Poochie, Doozer*, and *Hoopers*, and my brothers were *Punkin, Buddy*, and *Boze*. So Skeeter was a name that suited me just fine.

I was the oldest of the bunch. On the night I was born, a neighbor gave me a little dog named Snowball. He was a small white terrier and looked like the dog on the old RCA Victor records. Snowball followed me everywhere.

Back when this story takes place, my family lived in an old log cabin at the end of a country road. In the summers, when we got a downpour of Kentucky rain, that road was just mud. But we kids didn't mind much. Since we were living in the heart of the country, we never wore shoes from May to September anyway. We just let that rich brown mud squish up between our toes.

We always had a white Kentucky Christmas in those days. Come November, snowflakes would be fluttering down like millions of tiny white moths.

The Christmas I was ten years old, I wanted a doll more than anything else in the world. All summer long I had dropped more hints than a porcupine has quills. So I was pretty certain that Santa would not disappoint me. Hadn't I been good? Hadn't I helped Mother with the little kids? Hadn't I studied hard in school? Hadn't I even rescued a bluebird with a broken wing?

These were my thoughts, as the first snowflakes fell over Dry Ridge.

When the holidays finally rolled around, it was time to put up our tree. Christmas was only two weeks away!

As usual, finding the ideal Christmas tree was a big adventure. Daddy took his ax, the one with the handmade handle, and we children followed his footprints through the snow.

Buddy wanted a pine tree, with big thick cones hanging from the branches. Poochie thought we should choose an elm, since it looked so lonely without its summer leaves. But Daddy just shook his head.

"We'll know the perfect tree when we see it," he said. So, with Snowball at our heels, we kept on looking.

Finally, on the road running past an abandoned field, we came upon a cedar tree, standing all by itself.

"There it is, Daddy!" we cried out. "There's our Christmas tree!"

Decorating the cedar was another great adventure, especially when Mother got out her box of decorations. I tried to keep my thoughts away from that beautiful doll, but I could see her so clearly in my mind's eye! Only in the excitement of trimming our tree could I forget her.

"We'll put this up last," Mother said, as she unpacked a pretty yellow star that Granny Penick had made out of cardboard and cloth.

"Mother? Can I get the Wish Book now?" I asked, and she nodded. So I took out the Sears & Roebuck catalog—we called it the *Wish Book* back in those days—and we kids tore out the most colorful pictures we could find. Then we made paper ornaments out of the pages and put strings through them. The littlest kids hung them on the lowest branches.

Mother popped a pan of corn so that we could make popcorn strands. And then we added silver icicles and gobs of angel hair. That angel hair was feathery as goose down. I was sure that angels must brush their hair an awful lot to get it so soft.

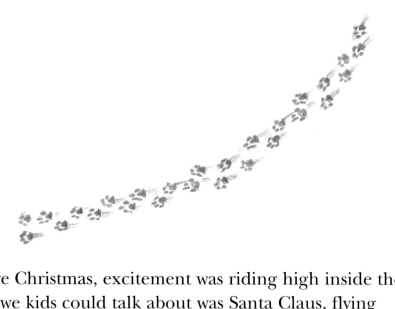

Two days before Christmas, excitement was riding high inside the little log cabin. All we kids could talk about was Santa Claus, flying through the dark Kentucky skies to reach us.

"Why don't y'all go on out and play," Mother said. "You're about to drive me crazy."

So we bundled into coats, pulled on our hand-knit mittens, and went outside to make angels in the snow. We made lots of them. I made BIG ones, while Poochie made little ones. The angels wore soft, fragile gowns made of downy snowflakes.

As we stood looking down at our angels, a wind started up in the trees. We closed our eyes, and that's when we heard the rustle of wings.

"Listen, Poochie," I whispered. "The snow angels are flying up to heaven."

On the day before Christmas we got out the bells that were hanging in the barn. Then we rang them just for the sheer fun of it! We didn't have any silver bells, like in the Christmas carol. But we had bells that the farm animals wore around their necks.

We stood outside our cabin and rang those bells until our hands hurt. I secretly hoped that Santa would hear the racket, all the way up at the North Pole. I figured the noise would help him and his reindeer find Dry Ridge. That way, my doll would be sure to arrive safely.

"Skeeter?" my brother asked, as he tugged on the sleeve of my coat. "Is this what the Bible means when it says to *make a joyful noise?*"

"Just ring your cowbell, Buddy," I told him.

Before we went inside to supper, we rang the bells one last time. And we stood and listened to the pure rich sounds as they echoed through the snowy mountains of Kentucky.

That night, Mother decided we would have a special treat. After all, it was Christmas Eve!

"How about some snow cream, kids?" she asked, and we went wild. You see, we didn't have a fancy thing like ice cream back in Dry Ridge, not in those days. So we made our own version at home. With us kids helping out, Mother got a kettle of snow from outside.

"I'll get the eggs!" Buddy cried, and raced out to the henhouse before Mother or I could stop him.

"Silly," I told him when he returned with four delicate eggs. "You don't put eggs in snow cream."

"We'll have them for breakfast," Mother said, as she poured milk, sugar, and vanilla into her big blue bowl. Since I was the oldest, she let me do the mixing. Soon we all had bowls of snow cream. It wasn't store-bought ice cream, but it was delicious.

As the oldest child, one of my chores was to get the little ones into bed. And since it was Christmas Eve, I didn't waste any time. I washed their faces, combed their hair, and then coaxed them into their pajamas. As I worked, I thought, "I'll be doing this for my dolly very soon."

Then, we all knelt to say our prayers. I don't know what my brothers and sisters asked for, but I put in one final request for that doll before I tucked them into bed. But they were too excited to sleep.

"Skeeter, sing us a Christmas song," cried Boze.

"Sing us 'Away in a Manger,'" cried Punkin.

"Sing 'I Wanna Be a Cowboy's Sweetheart,'" cried Poochie.

Sing 'What Will We Do with the Drunken Sailor,'" cried Buddy.

I took a big breath, and then sang them a whole bunch of songs until their eyelids got heavy. Soon they were snoring like little mice. Then, I tiptoed downstairs to say goodnight to Mother and Daddy.

"Come here, honey," my daddy said. He was sitting in his favorite rocking chair, so I climbed into his lap. "Are you all ready for Santa Claus?"

"I sure am, Daddy," I answered. I glanced over at my mother and smiled. I saw a funny, secret look pass between her and my daddy. Mother put her knitting down and came to brush my hair.

"Remember this, Skeeter," she said. "Sometimes, we don't get all the things we wish for. But gifts come in all shapes and sizes. This family has a lot to be thankful for. There are folks worse off than we are." I knew this was true. I had seen the relief workers who arrived every holiday, bringing presents to the kids who would have none otherwise. There was even a popular song on the radio, by the legendary Mr. Eddy Arnold. It was called "Will Santy Come to Shanty Town?" So I sang part of it for Mother and Daddy.

> *Now if I say my prayers each day,*
> *'Til Christmas rolls around,*
> *Will Santy come to Shanty town?*

"See, Mother?" I said. "I know about those folks poorer than us. And I'm real thankful for what we got." She just smiled down at me.

"Get yourself up to bed now," Daddy said. "Before you know it, it'll be Christmas morning."

17

It was snowing hard when I went up to bed. A strong wind from the Plains was blasting its way through Kentucky. So I knelt by my bed and said an extra prayer for Santa Claus. I even prayed that his reindeer would have plenty of food and water to get them through the night. Then I crept under the warm covers.

But falling asleep is never easy on Christmas Eve. I lay awake, watching the gusts of snow as they beat against my window. I worried that Santa might not make it to Dry Ridge in such a storm. I knew he had a long way to come, all the way from the North Pole to Kentucky. But I also had faith that he'd make it. And the doll he would bring me would have long blond hair and blue eyes, just like me. I even knew what I would name her: *Leona Naomi*, after my beloved grandma.

When I finally did fall asleep, I woke often. I heard every creak of the log cabin, as it settled down for a long, cold night. If a mouse had sneezed, I would have heard it. If a spider had dropped down on a strand of web, I would have stirred in my dreams. Each time Daddy tended the fire, I sat up in my bed.

"Santa?" I whispered. "Is that you?"

But my only answer was the wind, as it rattled a loose board on the barn's roof.

I must have fallen asleep, because before long I heard the old rooster crow. I knew that dawn had come, and with it Christmas morning! I rubbed the sleep from my eyes and hurried to wake the little kids.

We all knew that we'd find nuts and candy and apples and oranges under the tree downstairs. And that was an exciting present for us. You see, we kids never got to eat any fruit all year long. Oh, the year my sister Doozer was born, Daddy brought grapes home so we could celebrate the birth. But that's the only time I can remember getting fruit when it wasn't Christmas. So we knew a special treat waited for us. We also knew that we were to share whatever was under the tree.

"But this Christmas will be different," I thought, as I pulled the warm blankets off Buddy and Punkin and Boze. "I'm big enough now to have a gift all to myself."

Still I made a promise right then and there. I would let my little sisters play with Leona Naomi. And then we all scrambled down the stairs.

There sat our beautiful cedar tree. The winter storm was over and the morning sun bounced off the silver icicles. The angel hair was scattered on the branches like freshly fallen snow. The popcorn strands looked good enough to eat. And the paper ornaments hung perfectly from each and every branch.

My heart was beating wildly. I thought it might fly away, like the bluebird I had rescued that summer.

"I wonder what Santa brought last night?" Daddy asked. Then he winked at Mother.

"Look under the tree, y'all," Mother said. So we got down on our knees and looked. I saw a Red Flyer wagon, loaded with oranges and apples and nuts and candy.

"Oh, the kids are gonna love this wagon," I thought, as I rolled it out from under the tree.

While Boze and Punkin and Buddy and Poochie and Doozer were admiring the Christmas treats, I peered back under the cedar.

"Leona Naomi must be very small," I thought. "But that's okay. Even little dolls deserve a lot of love." But there was nothing there. That bluebird in my heart started fluttering again.

I turned and looked up at my mother and daddy, a big question in my eyes.

"Oh, Skeeter, I almost forgot," said Mother. "Santa left something else."

"And it's just for you," Daddy added.

They pointed to a piece of paper that had been pinned to one of the branches.

My fingers trembled as I reached for the paper. With everyone watching, I carefully opened it. There, in a plain handwriting, was a message from Santa Claus.

Dear Skeeter, I am so sorry, but I ran out of dolls before I got to Dry Ridge. Santa knows so many little girls from all over the world who wanted dolls, too. And the elves can only make so many. I hope you will understand.

Love, Santa

"My, my, Sarah, just take a look at that," Daddy said to Mother. "It looks like Santa left Skeeter her very own Christmas note."

"Yes, William Lee, I see that," said Mother. "You're a lucky little girl, Skeeter. I bet you're the only child who got a note from Santa Claus."

My little brothers and sisters gathered around, giggling and grabbing at the paper.

"Let us see!" they cried.

I pretended to be happy. I smiled as I tucked the note into my shirt.

"I gotta go feed Ginger and Jenny and Mabel," I said, and reached for my coat.

Out in the barn, I gave our horse, Ginger, a nice breakfast of oats. I poured some cracked corn on the floor for the pigs. I climbed up the ladder to the loft and tossed down hay for my goat, Jenny, and for Mabel, the cow.

Then I climbed back down the ladder and threw myself onto the barn floor. And I cried my eyes out. My heart was broken. I was certain that I was the only girl in the world who didn't get a doll from Santa Claus.

As I lay there crying I heard a soft movement in the barn. I opened my eyes. There stood all the animals, peering down at me with curious faces. Snowball was there, his head tilted as he listened to my sobs. My cats, Luther and Minnie, squinted at me with sleepy, yellow eyes. Our rooster, Jake, was no longer strutting. Ginger had forgotten about her oats. Jenny and Mabel had stopped eating their hay.

All the animals were asking me what was wrong.

I sat up and looked around me. I looked at the horse, the pigs, the cow, the goat, the cats, the dog. I looked down at the soft yellow hay that padded the floor beneath me. I looked up at the blue sky through a crack in the roof.

And that's when it hit me. This day wasn't just about getting *gifts*. It was meant to celebrate the birth of a special person.

"Jesus was born in a lowly manger, on Christmas day," I said to the animals. Mabel lifted her head, and Jenny bleated softly. And then, as the animals listened, I sang them my favorite Christmas carol:

> *Away in a manger,*
> *No crib for His bed,*
> *The little Lord Jesus lay down his sweet head.*
>
> *The cattle are lowing,*
> *The poor baby wakes,*
> *But the little Lord Jesus, no crying he makes.*

"It's Christmas!" I shouted out. The animals all peered at me curiously. "Merry Christmas, y'all!"

I took the note out of my pocket and read it again. I was happy that all the other little girls in the world had gotten dolls from Santa Claus. I had *a Christmas note*, the only one of its kind!

I went back inside the cabin and I thanked Mother and Daddy for that Red Flyer wagon full of special treats.

And do you know what? For a lot of years my little brothers and sisters rode in that red wagon while I pulled them about. We got a lot of mileage out of that Christmas present.

Mother and Daddy never knew this, but on that stormy Christmas Eve so long ago, I woke in the night to the sound of voices. Certain that Santa Claus had finally arrived, I crept down the stairs to spy on him. I was hoping to catch him, just as he put Leona Naomi under the cedar tree. Instead, I saw Mother and Daddy sitting at our kitchen table.

I'm sure that Mother and Daddy knew Santa Claus personally. Thinking back, I suppose that he must have told them there would be no doll for me that Christmas. I suspect they already knew about the Christmas note. But they left Santa some biscuits and a cup of coffee anyway.

If I remember correctly, it was bitter cold that night. So I'm glad that they did.

It wasn't until years later, long after I'd left Kentucky to become a country singer, that I realized the true gift I had received that morning. It came in the shape of a Christmas note, with its sweet and simple handwriting.

These days, my home near Nashville, Tennessee, is filled with dolls from all over the world. These dolls are for the little girl who still lives inside me. But I often find myself thinking back to those nights of oil lamps and candles. I remember those December days when we kids plodded behind Daddy, stepping into his tracks with our tiny feet. I can smell the pure smell of cedar when I remember.

And then I think of Mother making us snow cream, and I can taste the sweetness of it on my tongue.

When I hear silver bells ringing out at the Grand Ole Opry each Christmas, I remember those plain old cowbells. "Yes, Buddy," I whisper. "They sure do make *a joyful noise.*"

Sometimes, if I listen carefully, I can still hear the rustling of angel wings. "See, Poochie?" I say aloud. "The snow angels are flying up to heaven."

Mother and Daddy have gone on to a better place now. But each year, when Christmas Eve rolls around, I get to thinking of the children who are waiting up for Santa Claus. Some of them will get all the gifts they've ever dreamed of. But others will not. That's when I feel that little bluebird rise up in my heart and try to fly away.

So, here is a Christmas message from me. It's for the child who lives in all of us, no matter what our ages. Remember these words, deep inside your heart, for those times when you might need them:

I am a special child of the world.
I am a great gift to the planet Earth.
I will live and grow and smile.
The day will come when I will be all
that I ever dreamed of being.

This is your own Christmas note. Remember, gifts come in all shapes and sizes. So tuck these words away, in that special place where only bluebirds can fly high enough to reach them.

Merry Christmas!